Chrysanthemum

by Kevin Henkes

Greenwillow Books

New York

FOR AVA

For information address HarperCollins Children's Books,
a division of HarperCollins Publishers, 10 East 53rd Street, New York, NY 10022
Printed in U.S.A.
www.harperchildrens.com
First Edition

11 12 13 WOR 30 29 28 27 26 25

Watercolor paints and
a black pen were used
for the full-color art.
The text type
is Cheltenham.

Library of Congress
Cataloging-in-Publication Data

Henkes, Kevin.
Chrysanthemum / by Kevin Henkes.
   p.   cm.
"Greenwillow Books."
Summary: Chrysanthemum loves
her name, until she starts
going to school and the other
children make fun of it.
ISBN 0-688-09699-9
ISBN 0-688-09700-6 (lib. bdg.)
ISBN 0-688-14732-1 (pbk.)
[1. Names, Personal—Fiction.
2. Schools—Fiction.]
I. Title.
PZ7.H389Cj   1991
[E]—dc20
90-39803   CIP   AC

The day she was born was the happiest day
in her parents' lives.
"She's perfect," said her mother.
"Absolutely," said her father.
And she was.
She was absolutely perfect.

"Her name must be everything she is," said her mother.

"Her name must be absolutely perfect," said her father.

And it was.

Chrysanthemum. Her parents named her Chrysanthemum.

Chrysanthemum grew and grew and **grew.**
And when she was old enough to appreciate it,
Chrysanthemum loved her name.

She loved the way it sounded when her mother woke her up.
She loved the way it sounded when her father called her for dinner.
And she loved the way it sounded when she whispered it to herself in the bathroom mirror.
Chrysanthemum, Chrysanthemum, Chrysanthemum.

Chrysanthemum loved the way her name looked when it was
written with ink on an envelope.
She loved the way it looked when it was written with icing
on her birthday cake.
And she loved the way it looked when she wrote it herself
with her fat orange crayon.
Chrysanthemum, Chrysanthemum, Chrysanthemum.

Chrysanthemum thought her name was absolutely perfect.
And then she started school.

On the first day, Chrysanthemum wore her sunniest dress
and her brightest smile. She ran all the way.
"Hooray!" said Chrysanthemum. "School!"

But when Mrs. Chud took roll call, everyone giggled upon hearing Chrysanthemum's name.

"It's so *long*," said Jo.

"It scarcely fits on your name tag," said Rita, pointing.

"I'm named after my grandmother," said Victoria.

"You're named after a *flower*!"

Chrysanthemum wilted.

She did not think her name was absolutely perfect.

She thought it was absolutely dreadful.

The rest of the day was not much better.

During naptime Victoria raised her hand and informed
Mrs. Chud that Chrysanthemum's name was spelled with
thirteen letters.

"That's exactly half as many letters as there are in the *entire*
alphabet!" Victoria explained.

"Thank you for sharing that with us, Victoria," said
Mrs. Chud. "Now put your head down."

"If I had a name like yours, I'd change it," Victoria said
as the students lined up to go home.
I wish I could, thought Chrysanthemum miserably.

"Welcome home!" said her mother.

"Welcome home!" said her father.

"School is no place for me," said Chrysanthemum. "My name is too long. It scarcely fits on my name tag. And I'm named after a *flower*!"

"Oh, pish," said her mother. "Your name is beautiful."

"And precious and priceless and fascinating and winsome," said her father.

"It's everything you are," said her mother.

"Absolutely perfect," said her father.

Chrysanthemum felt much better after her favorite dinner
(macaroni and cheese with ketchup) and an evening filled
with hugs and kisses and Parcheesi.

That night Chrysanthemum dreamed that her name was Jane.
It was an extremely pleasant dream.

The next morning Chrysanthemum wore her most comfortable jumper. She walked to school as slowly as she could.
She dragged her feet in the dirt.
Chrysanthemum, Chrysanthemum, Chrysanthemum, she wrote.

"She even *looks* like a flower," said Victoria, as
Chrysanthemum entered the playground.
"Let's pick her," said Rita, pointing.
"Let's smell her," said Jo.

Chrysanthemum wilted.
She did not think her name was absolutely perfect.
She thought it was absolutely dreadful.

The rest of the day was not much better.

During naptime Victoria raised her hand and said,

"A chrysanthemum is a flower. It lives in a garden with worms
and other dirty things."

"Thank you for sharing that with us, Victoria," said Mrs. Chud.

"Now put your head down."

"I just cannot believe your name," Victoria said as the students lined up to go home.

Neither can I, thought Chrysanthemum miserably.

"Welcome home!" said her mother.

"Welcome home!" said her father.

"School is no place for me," said Chrysanthemum. "They said I
even *look* like a flower. They pretended to pick me and smell me."

"Oh, pish," said her mother. "They're just jealous."

"And envious and begrudging and discontented and jaundiced,"
said her father.

"Who wouldn't be jealous of a name like yours?" said her
mother.

"After all, it's absolutely perfect," said her father.

Chrysanthemum felt a trifle better after her favorite dessert (chocolate cake with buttercream frosting) and another evening filled with hugs and kisses and Parcheesi.

That night Chrysanthemum dreamed that she really *was*
a chrysanthemum.
She sprouted leaves and petals. Victoria picked her and
plucked the leaves and petals one by one until there was
nothing left but a scrawny stem.
It was the worst nightmare of Chrysanthemum's life.

Chrysanthemum wore her outfit with seven pockets the
next morning.
She loaded the pockets with her most prized possessions
and her good-luck charms.
Chrysanthemum took the longest route possible to school.
She stopped and stared at each and every flower.
"Chrysanthemum, Chrysanthemum, Chrysanthemum,"
the flowers seemed to say.

That morning the students were introduced to Mrs. Twinkle,
the music teacher.

Her voice was like something out of a dream, as was everything
else about her.

The students were speechless.

They thought Mrs. Twinkle was an indescribable wonder.

They went out of their way to make a nice impression.

Mrs. Twinkle led the students in scales.

Then she assigned roles for the class musicale.

Victoria was chosen as the dainty Fairy Queen.

Rita was chosen as the spiffy Butterfly Princess.

Jo was chosen as the all-important Pixie-messenger.

And Chrysanthemum was chosen as a daisy.

"Chrysanthemum's a daisy! Chrysanthemum's a daisy!"
Jo, Rita, and Victoria chanted, thinking it was wildly funny.

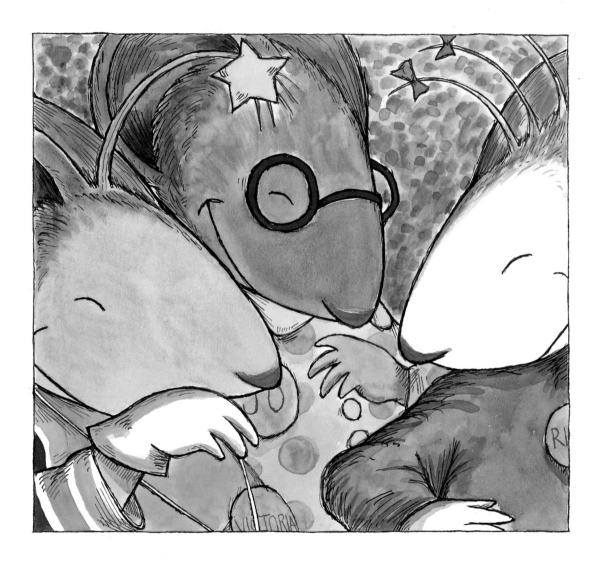

Chrysanthemum wilted.
She did not think her name was absolutely perfect.
She thought it was absolutely dreadful.

"What's so humorous?" asked Mrs. Twinkle.

"Chrysanthemum!" was the answer.

"Her name is so *long*," said Jo.

"It scarcely fits on her name tag," said Rita, pointing.

"I'm named after my grandmother," said Victoria.

"She's named after a *flower*!"

"*My* name is long," said Mrs. Twinkle.

"It *is*?" said Jo.

"*My* name would scarcely fit on a name tag," said Mrs. Twinkle.

"It *would*?" said Rita, pointing.

"*And*—" said Mrs. Twinkle, "*I'm* named after a flower, too!"

"You *are*?" said Victoria.

"Yes," said Mrs. Twinkle. "My name is Delphinium.
Delphinium Twinkle. And if my baby is a girl, I'm considering
Chrysanthemum as a name. I think it's absolutely perfect."

Chrysanthemum could scarcely believe her ears.
She blushed.
She beamed.
She bloomed.
Chrysanthemum, Chrysanthemum, Chrysanthemum.

Jo, Rita, and Victoria looked at Chrysanthemum longingly.

"Call me Marigold," said Jo.

"I'm Carnation," said Rita, pointing.

"My name is Lily of the Valley," said Victoria.

Chrysanthemum did not *think* her name was absolutely perfect.
She *knew* it!

EPILOGUE:

Overall, the class musicale was a huge success.
Chrysanthemum was absolutely perfect as a daisy.
Victoria made the only mistake: She completely forgot her lines
as the dainty Fairy Queen.
Chrysanthemum thought it was wildly funny, and she giggled
throughout the entire Dance of the Flowers.

Eventually, Mrs. Twinkle gave birth to a healthy baby girl.
And, of course, she named her Chrysanthemum.